Three Bridges

James Wilson

Three Bridges

A novella-in-triptych

Neverland Publishing
2014

.

Printed in the United States of America
ISBN 13:
978-0-9888290-60

www.neverlandpublishing.com

Though on Al-Sirat's arch I stood,
Which totters o'er the fiery flood,
With Paradise within my view

Byron, *The Giaour*

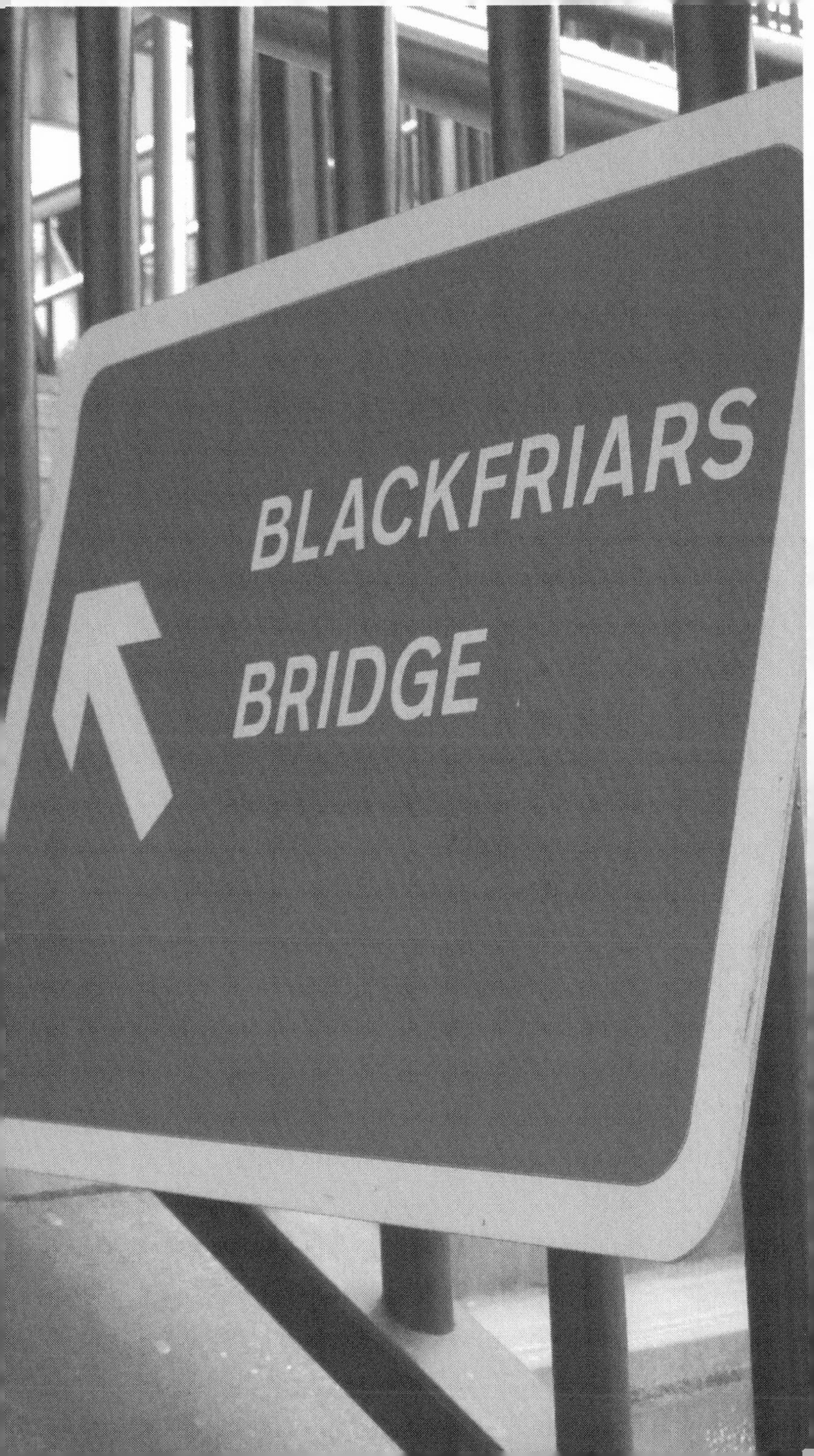
BLACKFRIARS
BRIDGE

Some time

I have become increasingly aware of the destruction and decay this world is made of. Beside the railway tracks, on the many train journeys I still have to take across the city, I see so much rusting metal, mouldy wood and eclectic detritus (ranging from rubber tyres to garden furniture) that I also find it hard to believe that anything ever disappears completely. There are grave-stones in decrepit cemeteries overgrown with bramble belonging to people whom no one living can remember, or possibly even care about, yet they stand and they remain, crooked maybe, illegible maybe, chipped and cracked and lichen-covered, maybe, but they stand and they remain. And the dust and bones beneath them, that remains too, it lingers like a doubt.

We seem to be caught between the Scylla of preservation and the Charybdis of destruction, doomed to forever be remembering something fading away.

And in the face of this slow process of erosion that will, seemingly, never be complete, I watch all the cycles of repetition, the routines with which we fill our lives, hoping, perhaps, to stave off or maybe even accelerate the disintegration of our selves. The repetition of actions and words can give comfort, a feeling of order and control, but at the same time the words and actions can become abrasive, wearing down meaning and intention the more they are repeated. I remember that one of my own cycles of repetition used to be one of my most frequent rail journeys: taking the northbound service into London, riding over the Thames and into Blackfriars station every Tuesday and Thursday afternoon as I went to see my representatives at the union.

I remember how I began to feel a sinking feeling in my stomach almost as soon as I saw the first glint of the river, how it was as if I was being slowly drowned from within. It had nothing to do with my compensation claim—although my case was going badly at that time—instead it seemed a presage connected to something both more remote and all-too immediate. Something that was both more remote and all-too immediate *then*; and something that continued to be, nay, continues to be (may, indeed, *always* be) ever more remote and all-too bloody immediate.

Sometimes I can feel the past rising up behind me like a great wave threatening to break and subsume everything. And at other times, in certain places of this city of mine, the past seems to bubble up and rise through the drains and manhole covers, seeping through the paving slabs of the very streets themselves, impeding my progress, just as it did at times when I exited Blackfriars station and crossed the road at the northern foot of Blackfriars Bridge. It was here that I once had a chance acquaintance with a woman I knew from an earlier period of my life. Amidst the endless flow of weaving, waltzing, strutting and darting people on the pavement, we were the only two stood still, waiting to

cross at a set of traffic lights. As pedestrians eddied around us, everso close but never making contact, she tapped me lightly on the elbow. I removed my headphones to find Catherine smiling at me, craning her neck forward as she did so. For an instant, it seemed as though we were in the middle of a conversation started in a different age and that she was expecting an answer to a question she had posed. I returned her smile and so began a series of customary pleasantries that resulted in us arranging to meet for a drink the following evening.

The pub was fairly deserted, save for a few mute individuals who sat apart from each other and stared disinterestedly at a screen showing a football match between Auxerre and Glasgow Rangers. After five minutes, to my relief and regret, Catherine arrived.

Gavin? Oh no, that ended soon after, Catherine said in response to one of my questions, asked some way into the evening when the caginess of the conversation had been moderated a little. I never felt guilty about what I had done, she said, whereas he only wanted to continue the relationship to make me feel guilty, to have some kind of hold over me. When he realized he couldn't get this, well, it just collapsed. And Catherine pushed the beer mat she had been scratching away from her. She fell silent for a few seconds before pulling the beer mat back to the edge of the table and continuing.

I say collapsed, but nothing's ever as sudden as that, is it? I mean, even years later, you can run into someone and feelings you thought were gone forever turn out only to have been dormant. Hitherto looking at the table, her hands, or the pathetic lights of the fruit machine, here Catherine decided to look me straight in the eyes with a force that bordered on the confrontational. There are always remnants, she said, you can never fully tear something up at the roots, and when he said he still loved me, I believed him. And when he said I still loved him, I almost wanted that to be true as well.

I had moved out at this point, temporarily perhaps, and was staying with my brother and his wife. In those uncertain days when it wasn't clear whether we were going to split up, were splitting up, or had already split up, he was invariably drunk and twice he hit me. The first time, I had gone back to the flat for one of those nebulous reasons that, I guess, we can only describe as our feelings. I don't know whether I hoped to patch things up or end things for sure. I don't remember what I said—at times like that, when you open up your heart, you think you are saying the most important words of your life—but it's the feelings that you remember.

It's funny, she said, although I could tell he had been drinking, I knew that when he hit me, it had nothing to do with the alcohol in his bloodstream, it was something he would have done in the most lucid of sobrieties, and Catherine looked slightly up and to the left, as though seeking some kind of verification from somewhere perhaps beyond even her ken. (It was the act of a desperate man, perhaps, trying to shatter of his own accord that which seemed to be fracturing irregardless of anything he could or couldn't do.) I didn't regret anything that happened, Catherine said. I still don't, she added, eyes momentarily glancing up from her hands on the table. But it was that night, at that moment even, that I realized I could truly hurt someone, that something I might do could affect others. This bond I had with humanity scared me, though it wasn't long before I was forgetting it and returning to a stage in which I was once more the leading player. Gavin phoned me up in tears and implored me to give him the chance to apologize in person, but the next time we met he hit me again. On that particular evening I watched him down shot after shot of whisky as he tried with increasing inarticulacy to explain just how much I had hurt him and how he loved me in spite of this and was prepared to forgive me. I said I didn't want his forgiveness. He said we could still work things out. It seemed pointless talking round in circles this way and I left. Against my wishes he accompanied me to my bus stop where he tried to kiss me. I turned my face away from him and he slapped me. It was less a violent action than a pathetic one and in a way I was grateful, for at least I knew it was finished now... or as finished as anything can be. I always thought that what I wanted was to feel needed. That's probably why from the age of thirteen until that very night I was never more than a few days without a boyfriend. But here I was rejecting the person who needed me, whilst the person I needed had rejected me, it seemed.

By the end of that week, Catherine continued, I had packed the rest of my clothes and rented a small one-bedroomed apartment that felt cold and claustrophobic. Living on my own and single for the first time in ages—Gavin and I had, of course, been living together for nearly two years—I had never felt so alone. Amazingly, Gavin became very reasonable and amenable towards me, he was fine with maintaining the lease on our flat alone and said I could have whatever furniture I wanted. He even offered to pay half for anything that I didn't want but that we had bought together.

I tried to spend as little time in my new apartment as possible, but was hardly outgoing. I worked late every night at the office, even sometimes at weekends, but still there seemed so much time to be filled. As you well know, I have always found it easier to get on with and make friends with men, usually from the social circles of my boyfriends—something which, I fear, has done me irreparable damage of a nature I do not know how to describe. Most of my friends I had, of course, inherited through Gavin and although they were all very understanding and eager for me not to feel that the situation was awkward for them, I felt a period of self-imposed isolation almost necessary.

It was then that the barman rang the bell for last orders and we decided to leave, shaking hands rather awkwardly as we parted. I boarded a bus and, after paying my fare, climbed the steps to the upper deck. Consumed by memories and staring blankly ahead of me, it was only when the vaguely familiar lights of the Odziller kebab shop pierced through my reflection that I pressed the bell and alighted, having missed my intended stop by some distance.

Two days later I received a text message from Catherine saying that she would like to see me again and continue our discussion. You can choose where and when the message informed me, in abbreviated terms.

The following night we met at a bar near the library where I was researching. As I explained to Catherine, I had never been to this bar before, but had often passed it and found its darkness alluring, situated, as it was, in a basement. You've hardly changed a bit, she replied.

Returning from the bar with our drinks, Catherine sat down and let the strap of her handbag slip off her shoulder as she pushed my glass across the table to me. It wasn't long before our conversation returned to the place where Catherine had left off a few days before.

The months went by slowly and monotonously and to fill up time she started taking evening classes at the local community centre, she told me. I found my life governed by a solitude I was unfamiliar with, she said, the memory of the recent past trailing me like a shadow. I was never really alone—my

colleagues at work always showed the appropriate amount of interest and concern in me, as did my mum and my brother, who between them phoned often enough—but this kind of attentiveness only exacerbated things, made me believe that what I wanted from life was unobtainable or even preposterous. I think there is only one period of life where you find true happiness and after that everything else is simulated. You might meet someone new, but from the very start they are surrounded with a kind of penumbra. It obscures their true light and might never be cast off. And the frustrating thing is that it is not their baggage or prior existence that wreathes them in this dimness, but your own history and reference points, projected on to them ceaselessly, helplessly, leaving you not knowing what you're seeing, not knowing who you're fooling: yourself; them; or, the bygone other. One period of true happiness. The primogenitor from which a copy of a copy of a copy is made, each time fainter than the last, vibrancy and detail blurred away with use and time until all your feelings and experiences blend in to an homogenized and indistinguishable mass that could be shifted wholesale, backwards or forwards, along all subsequent eras of your life.

Have you never thought that? I shrugged my shoulders.

I chose one class that I thought of loosely as more academic, Catherine went on, and that was learning Japanese, and another that might be more practical, which was web design. Strangely enough it has turned out to be the other way round. After a few weeks I began seeing the teacher of the web design class, Steven. At first a drink after class, then we would meet up on other days of the week. I invited him to have dinner at my flat and it felt good to hear our voices there, as though the conversations were dissipating the haze of loneliness and self-pity which had previously coated those four walls. As I come to think of it, he nearly always came round to see me. Whenever I went over to the house where he was living, it was only ever to meet him before we would go on somewhere else. He was incredibly intelligent, almost intimidatingly so, in spite of the attempts he made to play his intellect down by constantly making all of his analogies in reference to daytime soap operas and annoying advertising campaigns. Steven was charming and somehow managed to always make me feel at ease, he was the first person I'd met in a while that I felt I could really talk to. He listened—and unlike others, he didn't just listen so that I'd have to reciprocate when it was his turn to have his say. He listened, it seemed, with a genuine desire to understand me. But perhaps that too was just another out-of-focus projection.

What did he look like, I asked.

Well, I guess he was about the same height as, er, Gavin, brown hair... not especially good-looking, but not bad-looking either.

It wasn't about that. Not this time. He reminded me of a priest somehow, Catherine laughed. He seemed so strong and so vulnerable at the same time. And she sighed, exhaling a boredom or lassitude that, one sensed, may have been present during our entire conversation, possibly, with one caesura, our entire lives. She looked at her watch, then over her shoulder at the dark and empty bar behind, searching for I know not what and probably not finding it. At length, she shifted back round in her chair.

It was after we'd been going out five or six weeks, she resumed, compelled to finish her tale (now begun, long finished, never ended), that I first noticed his racism. He didn't say anything to people, just these occasional comments to me, almost as if in passing, veiled at first, but then more overt. I didn't know how to react, perhaps he was testing me, and when I didn't say anything, perhaps he took that for some kind of assent. About a month later I found out he was a

member of the BNP, in fact, he had designed their website. He had kept this well hidden from most people and it was around the time that I found out that it became more public knowledge. He got abuse from a few people and, as news spread, it escalated. He received threatening letters, people began not to attend his classes; and then all classes were boycotted in protest, with petitions made to have Steven dismissed. It made the local news, both in the papers and the early evening television broadcast. In no way did I condone his views, but I was attracted to the role of defending him. I was not ashamed to be seen with him in public, but, although he was adept at talking about politics, he was no politician and I was no politician's wife. He retreated into himself. I wanted to be there so he could confide in me, the way I had so often bawled out my problems to him. But he said less and less, scared that there might be a word that might make me turn on him too. Then one day I received an email from him telling me that he didn't want to embroil me in what was his problem and that it was better for all concerned if we stopped seeing each other forthwith. Forthwith, that's how he put it. He resigned his job voluntarily was the official edict. And I haven't heard from him since. When I rang at his door another tenant told me he had left leaving no forwarding address. He vanished out of my life in a way that was all too familiar to me... only I guess his disappearance was more complete, Catherine said hesitantly, looking at me, or through me, as if, perhaps, seeking confirmation.

Again I threw myself into my work, she said, again I found myself postponing my nightly returns to my flat so as to spend as little time there as possible. I began to hang around with the old crowd once more and discovered that they had largely cast Gavin aside after his drinking had gotten out of control and aggressive tendencies had begun to punctuate his behaviour with increasing regularity. I felt no great relief at being able to socialize without running into Gavin, quite simply because I felt no great relief at socializing with any of them, in spite of all their warmth. It's horrible, I know, to talk about friendships dragging on and being unbearable… but when they only serve as links to a—I was going to say painful, but it wasn't always painful—when they only serve as links to a thwarted past, when they only seem to tend and revere memories and experiences that need to be forgotten—or at least forgotten just long enough to let one briefly breathe the air of the present—that's understandable, is it not? I always found it strange that I inherited these friends from Gavin... and you, and whilst I continued to be in their midst, you and Gavin had become exiles. Gavin because, well, in the end he just made himself so unpleasant, and you... I don't know why. Why did you cut yourself off like that? If anyone it should have been me.

Slowly I found myself reverting to patterns of solitude, Catherine continued after giving me time to speak. I would hang around coffee shops at stations, she said, using the free wifi, and I would go to the cinema a lot. I remember one week I went to see the same film at the same cinema five times, each time alone. I felt comforted by the ability to predict the scenes, though as soon as the film ended I would feel scared by the realization that I didn't know what was going to happen to me in the rest of my life. All that uncertainty and incomprehension. I guess I've always wanted my life to have the containment rather than the fantasy of a movie. I think that's partly why I've chosen to go to Japan, because it's a chance to bring down the curtain on this act of my life. And it seemed so apt that I should run into you again. Like resolution, only I know it won't be like that.

Three weeks after this meeting Catherine departed for her post in Japan. My Tuesday and Thursday afternoon appointments at my union continued for several months and I persisted in crossing the northern foot of Blackfriars Bridge at the same pedestrian crossing, hoping less, perhaps, to dilute any new resonance this routine had accumulated than to stimulate, perhaps, some form of callus. I don't think I was successful as, years later, when a commission caused me to frequent the St Bride Library, I found myself regularly in the vicinity of Blackfriars Bridge once again and I began crossing the road at the same crossing, like rainwater following the paths of rainworn fissures with no choice of deviation. Yet elsewhere so much in the area was chang-ing and had changed. The railway station was being redeveloped to become the first station to span the river Thames and during the construction work the builders were making use of the adjacent pillars of a former railway bridge. These pillars and abutments that once bore the tracks of the London, Chatham and Dover Railway had stood abandoned and forlorn since 1984 when the bridge was dismantled. Painted a shade of red that could only come from a previous era, these pillars had, at various times, seemed to me intrinsically ridiculous and absolutely necessary and from certain angles they came to resemble the figures of a school of men who had attempted to bury their heads in the sand, diving headfirst into the riverbed only to leave their red-stockinged legs helplessly exposed above the water's surface, vulnerable to the constant haranguing and derision of the elements. And then, unexpectedly, after many years of stoic redundance, bearing nothing but the dull heavy weight of absence, these pillars had been pressed into service anew, operating as support platforms whilst expansions were made to the newer (but nevertheless aged) railway bridge just downstream. So much had changed and was changing indeed. And I remember that I used to wonder if I should curse myself or rejoice at my own comparative lack of progression. And I remember that I used to wonder if I should think myself blessed or damned by my apparent inability to be insensate to all that had gone away but not yet entirely disappeared.

And I remember that I used to wonder. And I wonder that I used to remember...

Blackfriars Bridge is Janus-faced, it seems. On the eastern side it carries carvings of various seabirds on its pillars; on the western side are images of freshwater fowl. The two sets of ornithological ornaments are said to represent Blackfriars as a tidal turning point of the Thames. To me, however, the two faces it proffers both look backwards: one at what was; the other at what might have been; and neither tableau seems firmer or fainter than the other, both shimmering beneath the same gauzy light of speculation that can't quite leave anything alone.

LONDON BRIDGE

Later

I try to avoid crossing the river by London
Bridge, where possible. It has become,
for me, as for T S Eliot before me, a bridge
of the damned and undead. There are few
sights as dispiriting as this bridge at 8.30 in
the morning or 5.30 in the evening, the suited
masses hurrying to and from underground
and overground railway stations in scenes
little different to those of Fritz Lang's
Metropolis where the workers pour in or
out of the industrial god, Moloch.

Personalities, empathies, at times simple
decencies, all these are worn away by

commutes just started or soon to be ended; by the lingering or beckoning glows of computer screens; and the rictus of vacant swivel chairs and 'ergonomic' desks. In their stead are spectres, determined phantoms repeating the same runs and routes for vastations of unqualified lengths—perhaps never to be ended; perhaps to end all too soon, a certain umbrella adorned with a certain golf club crest seen every day then never again; a girl who sports overhead earphones passed each morning without acknowledgment, then vanished forever into the anonymity she had never properly emerged from, like the eyes and nostrils of a crocodile, sinisterly sinking back beneath the surface of a waterhole.

I am fortunate enough to have escaped this perdition many years ago now; a dispute in the workplace eventually affording me a generous compensation package and, perhaps more importantly, the chance to change careers and work for myself. The chance, also, to free myself from that twice-daily walk across London Bridge in the company of absent souls and errant hopes.

Throughout my life I have been unable to avoid looking backwards without covering the formerly traversed scenery in an almost affectionate shade of loss and longing (even those backdrops upon which bloodstains and salt tears have dried, leaving in their wakes visible and at times all-too visceral presences that can never be fully scrubbed away, only varnished and sealed in forever). But that walk of the damned over London

Bridge has proved to be an exception. It continues to provoke dread and nerves, but not once has it prompted loss or longing.

I now suspect that my aversion to the bridge was less to do with the misery I experienced both professionally and personally whilst making a commute to a job that I did not enjoy—nor the subsequent memories and unavoidable psychological linkings—but more to do with some vague sense of premonition that was lurking within me. A premonition that the bridge could be my undoing; that to walk its span was to leave myself vulnerable and exposed in a way that no other blind alley, broad boulevard, ornate square, station concourse, commercial high street, traffic rat run, residential road, public park, pavement terrasse or rooftop garden in this city ever could.

In time, I came to revisit the surrounding locales of my erstwhile employers, drawn in by the sense of my own fragmenting past as though by some irresistible scent. I felt no bitterness or anger or vindication and had, instead, begun to look back on some aspects of those few years of unhappiness with a feeling that resembled a dull and medicated curiosity. The benches around St Paul's Cathedral where I would sometimes sit and eat my lunch; the stretches of London Wall beside which I would smoke a cigarette, always captivated by the way

in which the remains of the wall seemed to have been dug out and revealed to preserve less their historical importance and centuries of age, but rather their forlorn and semi-permanent state of decay and decrepitude; the pub below Cannon Street station where I would sometimes go for a drink at the behest of my colleagues after work on a Friday evening, feeling lost in the oppressive atmosphere of money and machismo that I have since come to think of as one of the circles of hell—all these places associated with my three years as an office worker I had subsequently revisited in dazes of varying detachment, like some government inspector searching to determine whether contaminated land may now be habitable once more, the levels of radiation suitably diminished. But walking over London Bridge would continue to make me feel uneasy, and no amount of metaphorical or literal protective clothing could assuage my qualms. I did seek, I do seek, and maybe, trapped in a penitential ritual of my own creation, I always will seek to find other crossing points. Tower Bridge, Southwark Bridge and the Thames Path provide alternative pedestrian routes. Bank, Monument and Cannon Street stations offer Underground outlets and further insurances for my sanity or lack thereof.

My 'new' work—now years and years old, as stale and fetid as everything seems to become—sees me act as a freelance researcher; utilized by some well-known publishing houses to make preparations for a class of literary celebrity too busy or too lazy to engage from the start with the books that will later bear their names and furnish their incomes. Most of my work can be limited to a range of favoured library reading rooms across the capital, but, occasionally, I take on a project that requires me to conduct some original interviews.

It was just such a project—a book for a TV philosopher keen to tackle something on 'economics and emotions'—that saw me making my way into the City one January morning to interview employees at the London offices of a top NYSE-listed 'investment and asset management' corporation, hoping to gather the requisite amount of data from which a set of statistics could be extrapolated to help back up the television philosopher's half-formed theories of a correlation between levels of stress and a company's (perceived) questionable ethical record.

It was just such a project—a book for a philosophizing broadcaster, a book for a broadcasting philosopher, a book about economics and emotions, a book about emotional economics, a book that whichever way you turned it would never come to be written in any traditional sense of the word, the philosopher-author giving in to the narrow constraints of his own arteries before he could cast anything more than a cursory look at the documents compiled by me and the other researchers; the author-philosopher barely deigning to crease our pages or annotate our margins before succumbing to his most final word limit; but a book that was nevertheless published under his name two years after his death;

and a book that has gone on to boost the profiles and bank balances of a handful of editors described in some so-called learned reviews and journals as 'faithful' and 'honest'—it was just such an accursed project that saw me, one overcast January morning, once more crossing London Bridge on my way to work.

It was a short walk from London Bridge railway terminus to the investment company's offices on the west side of King William Street. A short walk and one that I would normally have foregone in favour of an unpleasant one-stop Tube journey on the Northern Line, had not services been suspended for the day due to industrial action taken by the RMT.

That morning the bridge was understandably even more busy than usual with pedestrian traffic and, as I joined the throngs, it felt like I was joining a current from which I might never emerge, like a branch of cork oak tossed into salivating rapids seeking to dash it to pieces or run it into oceans far from home. I bobbed and sailed along with the fast-moving flow of pinstripe, patent leather and pencil skirt, and immediately felt adrift from any remaining sense of normalcy. I passed a homeless man banging a set of drums improvised from upturned and emptied plastic vats of polyunsaturated cooking oils. Universally ignored, his rhythms were, nevertheless, universally obeyed, as he beat faster and faster, spurring the passers-by on to greater and greater feats of self-regard. I passed another man, his arms outstretched and proffering leaflets. Around his torso he wore a makeshift sandwich board that proclaimed his 15 years of IT expertise. His head was tilted up to face the grey banks of clouds; his eyes were closed and he might have been stood like that forever, undergoing a punishment devised by a set of listless Greek gods hidden somewhere up above or elsewhere out of sight. I remember how, as I weaved left and right to avoid the undeviating paths of hardened ashen-faced types intent only on the docks of their desks, I began to feel short of breath and somewhat vertiginous, and how it was with no small amount of relief that I disappeared down the steps of the subway on the northern bank of the river in order to cross over to the other side. In the passageway I caught the eyes of a *Big Issue* seller sat cross-legged and huddled beneath a tartan blanket. I think he might have asked if I was alright.

I never expected to view King William Street House as a sanctuary, but that morning it almost felt like one. Completed in 1976, the building squatted next to the bridge with an air of menace. It had always reminded me of (and, who knows, was perhaps even an inspiration for) a hybrid of assorted late '70s and '80s iconography: the logo of the fictional megacorporation Omni Consumer Products from the film *Robocop*; one of the indefatigable aliens

from *Space Invaders*; a Transformers toy
on the cusp of mutation; or the helmet and
black-visored eyes of one of George Lucas's
stormtroopers. It had a distinct lack of
humanity. But on that particular morning,

even immutable alien indifference seemed like an improvement. I showed the concierge my temporary visitor's pass and made my way up the stairs to the fourth floor where I had appropriately been given the use of a spare cubicle on the fringes of the human resources department.

I felt distracted during the course of the day, letting the interviewees prattle on and on to questions that I had forgotten I had posed as my gaze drifted out the windows and over the bridge, past a despairingly small sliver of visible river, and on towards the buildings on the southern bank, where I fantasized that someone was staring back at me, perhaps from out of one of the tinted windows of No. 1 London Bridge. This building was free of superstition in its thirteen storeys and, clad in stainless steel and flamed pink granite, it was something of a pin-up for 1980s postmodernist architecture. The glass-fronted façade, cut into the north-west corner of the building,

stared out from behind an imperious stiletto-like pillar, and even on gloomy days it maintained the ability to bear the ever-changing reflections of the city opposite, the skies above and the manifold contents of everything in between. If I was looking out at No. 1 London Bridge and wondering in some unformulated way about vanished, potential or parallel trajectories, well, perhaps it was apt, as not long ago I discovered that King William Street House and No. 1 London Bridge were linked in a manner that embodied and drew attention to just such absence, possibility, and hinting of alternative worlds. The façade of No. 1 London Bridge is supposed to line up with the south-east-facing alcove built into the main body of King William Street House in a configuration to mark the span of an earlier London Bridge.

Just now I said that I *discovered* this information, really I was *told* it. Taking pictures of King William Street House from across the river, I became conscious of a man hovering in my vicinity. Clothed in a dark blue mackintosh (though it had not rained all day, nor seemed like doing so) and sporting a well-groomed white moustache that sat above his upper lip like a foreign punctuation mark, he waited for me to put away my camera before approaching me. In perfect English, but with an accent that bore traces of a German, perhaps, or maybe a Czech upbringing, he told me about the ghost of a bridge that the two buildings continued to bear. He then pointed upwards and suggested I take a picture of a small but perfectly-formed cumulonimbus that could be seen, high above, framed

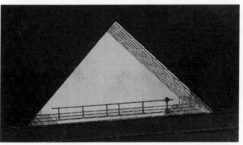

by the skylight cut into the overhanging corner of No. 1 London Bridge—a feature of the building that, I have to confess, I had hitherto been completely unaware of, in spite of having taken pictures of this edifice for some while. The man wandered off as I looked up at the cotton cloud and, though he couldn't have got very far in those few seconds, I failed to see his distinctive blue raincoat anywhere amongst the milling tourists, riverside runners, hospital visitors and office workers. Nevertheless, I liked what he had told me and I accepted it without much question. Such anecdotal hearsay, backed up by nothing save its own appeal, is, I have come to feel, a far surer and sturdier bedrock of our civilization than any of us realize, and underpins more of our actions, desires, creations, destructions, dreams and nightmares than any resort to empirical evidence ever will.

I don't know whether the man was referring to the medieval stone bridge that consisted of nineteen small arches and sported on its back a colossal weight of traffic, houses and shops—a real dense thicket of buildings that spilt over the sides of the bridge, spreading out above the slow-moving water of the Thames (sluggish from its forced working of mill wheels); buildings that also leant into each other in the other direction, over the actual roadway, like rugby scrummagers bearing the pack up in mutual antipathy and creating a crowded gloomy tunnel beneath. Or perhaps he was alluding to the later, nineteenth-century bridge designed by John Rennie, the Scottish engineer who specialized in bridges, canals, harbours and breakwaters. Such feats of construction always amaze me (even if the results leave me feeling cold) and I often think about the architects, designers, engineers, foremen and labourers who rarely live long enough to grasp what they have done; to see just how their creations go on to influence and be absorbed into the wondrous hideous patterns of lives both individual and collective. Their work is so often geared towards a future that they won't be a part of that they must continually feel themselves somewhat out-of-date or consigned to a past that is yet to actually happen. And when I see pictures of these people, these engineers of the future, trapped in the past, I look at them almost as at an entirely different species, amazed to ever see any mark of recognition or contemporaneity—such as the surprisingly modern haircut of John Rennie in the 1810 portrait by Sir Henry Raeburn—in their features.

I have pored over old charts and plans and I have studied countless engravings, drawings, photographs and landscape pictures from styles, schools and times as far apart as échoppe etchings from the Baroque period to Fauvist paintings of the Edwardian era (and many more from before and beyond), and I am still none the wiser as to which of the two bridges the man was referring to or whether, indeed, he intended some even earlier bridge, or perhaps another unrecorded one, of which no images remain and knowledge of which survives only in the most mysterious of ways.

As I looked out over the 'current' London Bridge, I remember, I felt the return of one of the headaches from which I had been suffering all that week, a pressure around the temples that, once first acknowledged, would maintain an almost vicelike grip, the pinching persisting for the rest of the day until it would evaporate at some unspecified hour of the evening, departing quietly and unannounced and leaving me suddenly feeling lighter and vaguely euphoric. True to the patterns and precedents already set—how difficult it seems, at times, for anything, illness included, to break out of even the shallowest rut, to emerge from even the slightest of slipstreams—the head-ache stayed with me, seeming to grow as the natural light dimmed outside and the harsh glare of the fluorescent strip light-ing, hung through the large tessellated panels of the false ceilings, grew more pronounced. It was dark by four o'clock and, my concentration levels having been dissipated almost entirely, I decided to cancel the last of my interviewees, rather than face another embarrassing incident, such as the one that had occurred during my questioning of a kind-faced member of the canteen staff, when my phone had rung and I had, on autopilot, taken it out of my pocket, but instead of answering it or switching it off, had just looked at its small screen with bewilderment, like a bird of prey that has just heard for the first time the high-pitched squeals of the vole it has pinned beneath its talons and is subsequently beginning to question the entire rationale of its being. After what must have been a long and awkward minute or so for her, the lady very gently touched me on the knee and asked whether I was going to take the call and whether, perhaps, I wanted her to leave. I apologized for my distraction and switched the phone off. At the conclusion to our interview I thanked her for her time and said goodbye, but five minutes later she returned, placing a mug of sweet tea on my desk that, she said, she thought I might need. I cancelled the final interview of the day and instead filled in the answers to my pre-prepared questionnaire myself. One of these made-up answers eventually appeared verbatim in the posthumously published book, the faithful editors apparently unconcerned at checking to what extent my transcriptions tallied with the tapes I had handed in at the same time. I can no longer remember the wording of the question—something about whether one felt the need to compensate, in other areas of one's life, for working for a company that had routinely faced accusations of supporting morally dubious activities—but the wording of the answer is still printed clearly on my memory. *For a long time I have worried that what I have* done, *my* actions, *so to speak, will be all that I will be judged upon. My intentions, thoughts and emotions discounted entirely in some final reckoning in which no excuses are possible, no matter how valid they may be. For all the foreboding this fills me with,*

I still struggle to reconcile this dread with anything I do in my professional career. I have always seen my job as a pillar of security in a life that is otherwise in constant fluxion. If I wasn't analysing tables of figures and making calculations here, I would probably be doing it somewhere else. And I don't see how, if that somewhere else was a small business or charitable organization, I just don't see how that would make me any more or any less culpable.

I started to type up some of my notes, making little progress as I tended, instead, to look at the strengthening reflections of the office and its staff that were now projecting out through the window panes and over King William Street and on to the bridge beyond without seeming to terminate anywhere definite, but, at certain angles, because of the double glazing, splintering into two slightly overlapping and distorted panoramas that did nothing to alleviate the throbbing at my temples, but did induce a saccharine nausea to rise from the pit of my stomach in sympathetic accompaniment. It was gone five o' clock when I was roused from my reverie, a strong wind buffeting the windows before the heavens opened and the rain lashed the glass like a set of impatient fingernails drumming upon the arms of a chair.

I closed down my laptop and packed it away into my bag along with my Dictaphone and my notes and an empty plastic bottle of water. I had neither overcoat nor umbrella with me and the RMT strike wasn't due to end till midnight. I only had to cross London Bridge to the rail station, but I was feeling apprehensive and reluctant. Not because of the rain—it was, for sure, getting heavier and, out on the bridge where the wind was free from the nuisance of buildings, the rain was being driven at the kind of acute angle that could soak a person to the bone in the shortest of times—no, it was not a concern for my clothes or my appearance or dryness that made me hesitate before riding the lift down to the ground floor to walk slowly across the polished ghost-veined marble floor. No, it was something else. Something unformulated and far more fearsome, it seemed. Eventually I emerged from the main set of revolving doors and into a slap of cold air. I lingered beneath the porch of No. 33 King William Street, not for the cover it afforded from the rain, but because I was feeling so weary that not only did my journey home seem intimidating, but even the very concept of home seemed awkward and overbearing. I suddenly felt incredibly isolated and abandoned, as though sensing a light (one that I could never see, hidden behind some closed door painted shut with no handles or means of admittance of any kind) had gone out with perfunctory abruptness.

I stood there on the porch for I know not how long, screwing my eyes shut to blackout the constant busy movement of all the workers dashing past me on the nearby

pavement beneath sombre umbrellas or folded copies of the *Evening Standard*. When I eventually tottered down the half-a-dozen or so steps from the porch to the pavement, I did so as though giving in to a force of destruction that would finish me as completely as it is possible to finish anything, a force of destruction that would hollow me out from the inside and then pinch my empty carapace until it shattered, like a discarded half of a pistachio shell, toyed with by the strong brute fingers of a bored and implacable being.

Almost as soon as I reached the pavement— I barely had enough time to orientate myself in a south-facing direction—I felt someone's shoulder crack into mine with a force that was impossible to ignore for both victim and perpetrator alike (for want of better words). I raised my hand in a vague apologetic gesture to the figure in the grey gaberdine coat who continued to move away, but nevertheless turned as he strode, to cast back over his shoulder a look of admonition and accusation—an attribution of responsibility for an accident I had no intention of causing and that, I felt, I could really do little about.

The neck rotated to reveal, over a shoulder still tensed with aggression, a face that had been in the process of mouthing words now vanished. I froze too, for here, by London Bridge, I stood face to face with one of the few entities I had tried to avoid more than London Bridge itself: Gavin. A man from a past I had failed to forget.

Gavin expressed his surprise and asked if I was ok. I don't know what I answered, or even if I answered at all, but I do remember that I briefly pinched the bridge of my nose between the thumb and forefinger of my left hand, and that I shut my eyes at the same time and saw an image of such clarity that it has stayed with me ever since: a string of bloody and serrated flesh floating and strung out vertically beneath the surface of otherwise placid waters. A hideous, but still captivating spectacle that I can only assume was some kind of visual representation of my own fraught state of mind, supplied by my hippocampuses and attached to my bubbling stew pot of feelings in such a way that I would never be allowed to forget them.

I can't quite remember how it happened—I seemed to surrender myself into Gavin's care and control like a hostage who knew that struggles were now redundant—but we were soon sat opposite each other in a booth by the window of a major-chain coffee shop by one of the entrances to Monument station. As we sat there and Gavin tore open a blue sachet of sugar, pouring it into the cap of frothed milk atop his coffee, I began to think how the Underground station beside us was once called King William Street, and was intended to be the City terminus of what would have been the world's first subterranean cable-car system. Instead it transpired that King William Street became a fixture on the City and South London Railway, the first deep-level electric railway and an early incarnation of the Northern Line, the 'Misery Line', black as black on the Underground map. The carriages that trailed behind the small yellow and black locomotives were windowless, the high-backed banks of cushioned seating within stretching up almost to the ceilings and earning the stock the nickname of 'padded cells'. It was reasoned that, as the trains were travelling through tunnels, there was nothing to see, and so no need for windows. But sometimes it is not a question of *what* or *whether* we see, it is just a matter of needing to *look out*, of needing to *look away*. Being sat squashed up in such a closed compartment, propelled along tunnels far beneath the surface of the earth, seemed to me to be a predicament so utterly helpless that I could scarcely believe anyone subjected themselves to it. But they did. The railway opened to the public in December 1890 and was flooded with 165,000 passengers in its first two weeks, and over five million in its first year of operation. Perhaps the people believed that, in confining themselves voluntarily and temporarily to these conditions of claustrophobic insanity, they were striking a form of wordless deal or pact that would limit the madness—the madness which we all, at some stage or another, fear has us in its sights—to the submerged parameters, allowing their lives on the surface up above to carry on in some manner of level-headedness, leniency and light. One can only come to the conclusion that such a bargain has failed on the scale of the personal, the universal, and at every step in between.

I remember remembering a trip to the London Transport Museum in Covent Garden as a child and how I must have seen and probably even boarded the 'padded cell' carriage they have on display there, a dark-wood cylinder that looks, from the outside,

more like a banister, stave or billiards cue
than a means of conveyance. And I now
recall the interior of the wagon, and how

it resonates with an atmosphere of gloom
that can not be leavened by the wax model
passengers arranged in an amusing mise-
en-scène, but instead wreathes these figures

with an unbearable otherness, rendering the whole exhibit into a kind of purgatorial waiting room, such as the train carriages full of suicides found in Frank Borzage's film adaptation of *Liliom.* I remember thinking the wax models preposterous; and the very notion of displaying large vehicles and entire units of transportation as archive items seemed likewise preposterous, as though we were looking at everything the wrong way through a lens; but then suddenly it seemed no more preposterous than me sitting in a café locked in between a faux-leather banquette, a Formica table top, and a man I hadn't seen in years who possessed a set of eyes so grey and serious that I had trouble looking at them from anything other than an oblique angle.

It's strange, Gavin was saying, but I'm glad to have run into you... literally. And where another man would have let out a laugh or at least some grunt of amusement or humour, he let out none. He explained that he wasn't angry—such a feeling had faded away many years ago—and that I needn't feel on edge. He stirred his coffee slowly and methodically. I knew where you lived, I knew where you worked, he said, if I had wanted to exact... he trailed off, tossing his spoon into his saucer with a tintinnabulation. Well, let's just say, he said, it would have happened by now. No, I am glad to have run into you because I feel that I have become so divorced from certain elements of my past that I have almost begun to wonder to what extent they happened, and to what extent they happened *to me*. For it oftentimes feels, when I remember that part of my life—and I have only recently started to do so—it often feels that it happened to a completely different person. A person I can barely comprehend and a person that I have little sympathy for. I have had no contact with anyone from that chaotic epoch, not Catherine, not Richard, not Leon, not anyone. And I have begun to wonder whether such an unequivocal and, admittedly, impossible, separation was unhealthy in ways that I am only just recognizing.

For the first time, I noticed the pressure around my temples lessen and I shifted my position on the bench, relaxing a little more into the booth and, in deed, into the situation as a whole. I suddenly seemed to know where I was and what I had to do. It was like all afternoon, all week, and perhaps for so much longer, I had been stuck in a cabin surrounded by countless knobs, buttons, levers and pulleys, an array that I had only ever thought of as a hindrance to mine ever finding any position of comfort, before realizing that this wasn't supposed to be a seat of leisure, but was a place of work, and that all of the pedals and switches were there not to confuse but to help me. To help me gain control; to help me gain control to a standard whereby I might finally discover the sequence of button pushings and lever crankings to find a way free from the overloaded dashboard and even to free myself from the very cabin itself.

Gavin was no different to the in-house lawyer I had interviewed earlier in the day. I had spoken to him two days previous when he had been abrupt and suspicious, viewing the exercise and my questions with contempt and as a waste of his time. Two days later he knocked on the corkboard panelling of my office cubicle and proceeded to open up in ways that none of my other interviewees had. His repeated use of the word 'mate', as he said goodbye, had left me feeling rather grubby. All I had to do was sit back and look out for certain visual indicators that would prompt me to prompt on. The sequence would reveal itself and I could yet escape.

Go on, I said. And Gavin went on. At times, he said, I think that the severance was a necessary one, and that it has helped me become a person who is far more comfortable in himself. A person who is, if

I am permitted to say so, a 'better' person, a more complete person. But I have started to have misgivings. To walk away from something, anything, someone, anyone, without turning around, well, I have a feeling that that is somehow unnatural. It is machine-like. And in recent months, as thoughts about my past have become more frequent, though always indistinct, flashing briefly across my mind like the blurred colours of a bird in flight, I have come to worry that my refusal to look backwards will only solidify and strengthen these mechanical aspects of my personality, perhaps setting in place an irreversible process of petrification that will prevent me, at some point in my life, from giving all that I have to give, from being all that I can be.

And of course, when I think about it now, he said, my shutting myself off from that part of my past wasn't as simple and straightforward as such a sentence or sequence of words might suggest. No, it was a messy business. A difficult situation to extricate oneself from. I'm sure you, of all people, can understand that. And I often wondered, back then, how you managed to disappear so successfully, as though you had just pressed a switch and were gone. Me, I yearned to yank the plugs out from their sockets, but it was impossible, the wires were all so confusingly intertwined. I would tug on one, and an entirely unexpected part of my life would be drained of power. The whole situation was, in many ways, said Gavin, a revelation to me. A revelation of my vulnerability and all the flaws that, I have since come to realize, make us such fascinating creatures. And Gavin made a gesture with his hand that may have included the café and its patrons, the world and its populations, or perhaps just my self and his self bound together in some category in his mind that he never went on to explain. My reactions at the time, he went on, were destructive and self-destructive.

I felt so stupid. Stupid and blind. A blind man regaining his sight to find that every prop and landmark by which he had been navigating his existence didn't just look completely different to how he had ever imagined them to be, but in fact looked completely disgusting, almost as if they had been especially designed to unlock the maximum amount of revulsion from within him, and from within him alone. But opposites need each other to exist, they yearn to consume each other and perhaps already share the same basic ingredients in their respective and constituent make-ups. Love and hate, good and evil, attraction and revulsion—they are concubines. Now that I could see again, I was fuelled by a burning desire, an ardent attraction, to consume or destroy the prime object of my revulsion. I couldn't let Catherine go. I was a horrible person, Gavin said, falling suddenly silent and looking down into the dregs of his cup with what seemed like an earnest contrition.

When she left, Gavin answered in response to a question I asked, it was almost a relief, as though I could relax into a clumsy, error-prone, self-destructive life without fear of breaking the one thing that I treasured above all else. Because although I longed to destroy her, that was only because I also longed to preserve and treasure her; the former was a constituent part of the latter, and the latter part of the former, as I have been trying, badly, to explain.

It didn't help that we had six months left on the lease of the flat, Gavin continued. Living in those rooms was less like living with ghosts and more like living in some kind of mortuary—every room, every item of furniture bearing upon it a corpse in some state of decay, clammy and cumbersome to deal with.

There was an anti-drinking and driving advertisement that ran at about the same time and was aimed at, and indeed aired, it seems, to me alone, Gavin said. I have never spoken to anyone since who has seen or remembers it. But it is firmly imprinted on my mind and can still send a shudder down my spine. A man sits down at his desk in his study and the well of the desk is occupied by the body of a dead child, still bearing the undried tracks of blood from the head wounds that cut short her life. He moves to his bed and the child's corpse is there beneath the covers. He opens the fridge and the limp and slender arm of the child drops down from one of the shelves, the finger nails purpled by pools of subcutaneous blood that will never flow again. I was drinking heavily, and I was drinking on my own, and the advert only ever seemed to play late at night when I was somewhat numbed from alcohol consumption and was drifting off in front of a television set that I had turned on, ironically, for company and some crumb of reassurance. That man was doomed to be plagued, wherever he went, by the death he had caused in a motor vehicle accident. And I thought, was I too due to be similarly confronted, everywhere I turned, by the wreckage of a horrifying collision?

I had also seen that advert, I thought, but didn't mention it to Gavin.

My drinking was destructive and self-destructive, I don't think there can be any doubts about that, Gavin said, staring at or through me in a manner that might have been deemed to encompass both defiance and remorse. But that changed after a couple of months, Gavin explained, when the opportunity arose to take up a position at his company's offices in Oxford. The timing worked out perfectly, said Gavin, with the expiry of the lease on the flat, and I was delighted to accept the transfer even though I had previously turned down two similar offers without any consideration at all, never once imagining living anywhere other than London. I began to think of everything in terms of 'exit strategy', counting down the days until my move to Oxford and the start of a new life and the chance to be a new person. A person free of the hurts, frustrations and vulnerabilities that had become so freshly apparent to me. Also, a person free of those negative and domineering traits that may have contributed towards those same hurts, frustrations and vulnerabilities. My exit strategy saw me planning to ditch every aspect of my life that reminded me of Catherine. The flat would go and the furniture with it. Friends were dropping away of their own accord, but those I did still see I was confrontational, obnoxious and downright unpleasant towards, both verbally and physically (if I felt needs be). It was a deliberate sabotage and when I left for Oxford I did so without turning back. And until recently that is how I have continued to live, marching forwards into my new life, hoping that certain plots of land behind me would revert to scrubland, becoming so overgrown, in time, as to be unrecognizable. It is only over the last few months, since I have become engaged and my fiancée and I have begun to plan our wedding for next year, that I have started to have vague thoughts and concerns about my past. And now, running into you, I am not concerned at all. I know that I can turn around any time I want to, there is nothing for me to be afraid or ashamed of any longer. The land is not entirely overgrown, but it is not entirely recognizable either—it is just background that I am happy to ignore in favour of the beautiful vista opening up in front of me. And I wish you luck. I look at you now and I wish you luck.

And with that Gavin slid out from his side of the table and in a couple of brisk paces he was out the door and gone.

SOUTHWARK BRIDGE.

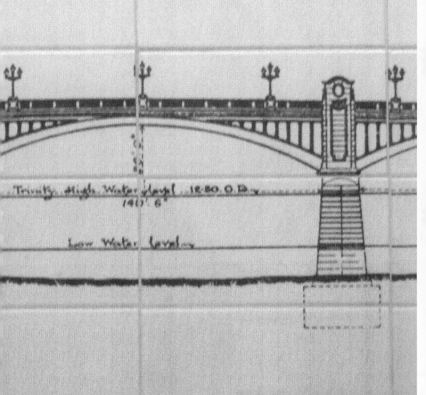

Trinity High Water level 18·80. O.D.
140' 6"

Low Water level

Later still

I have never quite been able to fathom how people fade in and fade out of one's life. They seem to be borne upon currents one has no control over, sometimes flashing past all too quick, never to be seen again; sometimes being washed up on our shores never to be dislodged; but more often than not, they come and go periodically, creaking for a while with the insistence of an aged shop sign spinning round and round in the wind, then falling suddenly silent, only to start up again, who knows when, and with some new whirring rhythm, just as though they had never stopped before.

I guess that Chris was, for me, a prime example of such a rusting weather-beaten sign. We once worked together during a period of my life now distant by some while. We saw each other five, six, even seven days of the week for three years; then not once for at least as lengthy a span. And now we meet up every now and again in an admission that we will never truly be able to shift each other from out of our respective lives, not that we, necessarily, desire to do so.

We are the stains that we hold in greater affection than the pieces of furniture we once thought we had ruined.

Chris still worked for the same City-based company that had once chewed me up and spat me out. When he discovered that I was working one day a week at the Guildhall Library, just a strong-armed stone's throw from his offices, he emailed me to suggest that we meet for a drink after work some time. He mooted the pub below Cannon

Street railway station where we had often drunk before, in a more youthful era of our lives. And so I found myself going to meet Chris for a beer or two on occasional Wednesday afternoons—when his schedule was conveniently uncluttered and mine own was as lacking in urgency and direction as ever—at a riverside watering hole I had once detested but was now coming to view with a certain begrudging affection and nostalgia, as though, just because it

had risen back from out of the depths of my past, it must have been missed and its return duly welcomed.

On one such Wednesday afternoon our conversation turned to the subject of a 'landmark' birthday party thrown by a mutual acquaintance on the preceding weekend. I had missed the party, being required to attend the book launch of an anthology of short prose and fiction that I had co-edited for a small arts publisher in Manchester on the vague theme of getting or being lost. I was sorry to have been absent from Leon's birthday festivities, for he was a man whom it was impossible not to hold dear to one's heart and the forwarded electronic flyer for his party had come with a personal addendum that had intrigued me greatly. Chris, however, had been able to attend and was keen, in due course, to tell me all about it.

Leon, Chris explained, has always been a man who cares little for petty squabbles and needless animosity, for divides and divisions of any sort. Sometimes this comes across as an admirable character trait, a magnanimous and generous attitude that is inclusive and embracing, not exclusive and hating. But sometimes I have come to see it, said Chris, as a mere side-effect of his incredibly blinkered and solipsistic world view, a world view that is, nevertheless, in its utter naïvité (or, as I am increasingly beginning to wonder, in its *horrifying truth*), both infectious and charming. People pop into his head and it is as though he is bringing them to life. They do not exist outside of his thoughts of them. The world sleeps when he sleeps, the world wakes when he wakes, and so forth, said Chris, looking at me for a nod or gesture of recognition and understanding. And so, Chris went on, he had sent out invitations for his party, across a range of media, to anyone he could remember, from any epoch or compartment of his life, as though time, absence, conflict and lack of familiarity were all completely irrelevant factors.

I arrived at the cavernous venue, the basement floor of a bar and restaurant off Borough High Street, and quickly ran into Leon. He disarmed me with a smile, a warm embrace and some platitudes before seamlessly introducing me to his friend, Peter, whilst at the same time managing to excuse himself from the pair of us to go and greet another couple of guests—a magpie forever flitting after newer shinier baubles.

As Peter explained how he knew Leon, I surveyed the room and began to feel slightly ill at ease, soon realizing that I knew almost none of the many faces I could see sat down around the wooden tables and recycled casks set into the nooks, recesses and vaults of this converted wine cellar. I recognized none of the laughing, chattering and smiling faces that were flickering in and out of the lapping shadows cast by candlelight, save a girl Leon had gone to college with whom I had met twice before over a ten-year period, and whose name I could not now remember.

As Peter blathered on, in the most amiable of fashions, about coming to know Leon through his work as a graphic designer, I felt myself sinking into or shrinking from, shrinking from or sinking into the unappealing prospect of an evening of continual politesse and small talk, of constant explanations and back stories. The kind of evening where one almost felt pressed to justify how, why and if one existed. An evening, ultimately, of exclusion. And I briefly wondered if it had been Leon's intention to invite the most disparate circles of people possible so that each would remind the other, over the course of the evening, that they would never belong to Leon's world in any but the most superficial of ways, and, by process of extrapolation, that they would never belong to anyone's life at all.

It was then that I spotted Gavin, said Chris, standing in the doorway and scouring the room with the same look of alienation and apprehension that I myself was feeling so keenly.

Now, I think, sometimes, Chris digressed, that we can confuse recognition with attraction. I don't necessarily mean sexual attraction—certainly not in this case—though of course this confusion happens in sexual relations too (especially those initiated under the haze of alcohol), but what I mean is simply a *positive drawing force*, for want of some better phrasing. We see someone we recognize and, I think, we are instinctively drawn to them. Usually, we are surrounded by hundreds of things we recognize, and we then place these things and people and qualities in orders of preference, in ever-changing hierarchies of attraction. But, rarely, we find our selves out of our depths, deep in alien terrains, and we latch on to anything at all that looks familiar. It is only later that we remember that recognition and familiarity work just as well with things we loathe or fear or lament as with things we love and respect and cherish.

I laughed for I knew just what Chris had meant. And I took advantage of the small lacuna created by this unexpected outbreak of levity and I got up to fetch us two more pints of generic lager. I made my way from our customary seats beneath the railway bridge overlooking the relentless Thames and went down to the sparsely populated bar below—a bar somehow made to seem all the more empty by the stream of chart-friendly music that was being piped in at such a negligible volume. The droves of office workers wouldn't start arriving for some time yet and the pub was bathed in an air of truancy and leisure time. There were a couple of tourists finishing a late lunch and from somewhere on the mezzanine up above emerged the sounds of a vibrant pool game being played by two off-duty street sweepers (I had noticed their carts left unattended in Steelyard Passage on my way in), the pleasing clackings and caroms of their contest being occasionally punctuated by the roars of their laughter and their celebratory shouts.

I enjoyed being at the pub at this time of the afternoon. It felt like *slipping away*. Slipping into some barely delineated zone where the regular conventions and yokes of life need not be applied with such remorseless rigour... at least just for a while. Slipping away from what, I don't know. From whom, I don't know either. But it felt like I had somehow snuck out behind my own back to be there. And I wondered if that sensation of leisure and escape, of tourism even, I wondered to what extent it was connected to our location, to some residue of its past that we had perhaps disturbed, releasing invisible spores into the atmosphere that might slowly have come to infect the patrons—in the course of their unthinking respiration—with some manner of alterity. For the pub was situated on land that had once formed a sort of fiefdom or independent country in miniature and could we, in a nebulous way, therefore be said to be haunted by the ghost of being abroad? Could we have stepped into the shade of a vacation? A brief holiday from London and the everyday limitations it tended to impose upon our thoughts and hopes and desires?

The faded foreign realms we were relaxing in were those of a former trading station of the Hanseatic League. The Hansa towns of Cologne, Lübeck and Hamburg had consolidated their London interests as far

back as the thirteenth century, establishing a base in the Dowgate ward of the City that had been called the Guildhall of the Germans or the Easterlings' Hall, before eventually coming to be known as the Steelyard following expansion of the grounds in 1474 as a result of the Treaty of Utrecht. The Steelyard took its name not from any connections to metalwork, but from the fact that on this spot had once stood the scales (or still) of the City of London, upon which every good had to be weighed. The pub we were in and Cannon Street railway station, overhead and beyond us, were built upon this former Teutonic enclave which nestled between the now submerged river Walbrook, to the west, and the disappeared All Hallows the More Church, to the east.

The community barricaded itself behind high walls and secure doors, and behind this fortress-like façade there played out, according to one historian, a mingled

record of all passions and interests, hates and favours, a veritable concoction of envy and enmity, honour and prosperity, greed and poverty, pride and fear, betrayal and reconciliation, manipulation and control, truth, corruption and deceit, in a word, a most motley record of which it is not easy to frame the contradictory elements into one harmonious picture.

The merchants and traders of the Steelyard were granted enormous privileges and effectively operated outside of English law. They were, at times, hated and persecuted by their English neighbours and during the Peasants' Revolt of 1381, all those who could not say the words 'bread' and 'cheese' properly were ruthlessly murdered by the rebels who had swarmed into the streets of London from the outlying counties of Essex and Kent, two places that have struggled ever since to conceal the virulent xenophobia that beats at their cores.

The Hanseatics lived secluded lives, in many respects, practising a monasticism devoted to business and the accumulation of wealth, and the traders were even bade to remain unmarried whilst resident at the

THE STEELVARD, LONDON. *(From an old Print.)*

Steelyard. But they became an accepted feature of London life, and the Steelyard became a welcome diversion from it. Between its riverside wharves, towered over by a huge lifting crane, and the high-gabled roof of its imperious Guildhall, there ran a pleasant garden planted with fruit trees, vines and currant bushes. Here the merchants might play at bowls upon the lawn or else seek the privacy of one of the many arbours. There were tables and chairs outside for customers of the Rhenish Wine House, a garden restaurant that was a popular destination for Londoners who wanted to slip away for just a while, to loose themselves from out of the ordinary and into the other. And perhaps this is what was persisting and pervading. And it felt like I should savour this sensation of escape because it could only ever be short-lived.

Well, I saw Gavin, Chris continued on my return from the bar, and it was like, after years of living abroad, spotting some lines of text in my native language. It didn't really matter what they said, whether they were a boring list of ingredients or the midrashim of a mystic, even if they were a stream of the most vile and obscenity-filled invective, my mind was eager to devour them. So I apologized to Peter, leaving his tale of poster artwork to freeze up and splinter in mid-air, and made my way over to Gavin.

After enthusiastic greetings were exchanged, we stood looking at each other, heads nodding excessively and faces smeared with achingly overdone smiles. We threw out some hesitant queries—queries not yet demanding of answers, but just limbering up, performing conversational stretches, so to speak.

As the *how-the-devil-are-yous* and the *I'm-great-and-yous* were knocked back and forth, I saw out the corner of my eye a table open up on the far side of the bar, and I suggested—instinctively, before I could even think what I was doing—I suggested to Gavin that we go and nab it.

We sat across from one another and that initial recognition seemed to wilt. I began to worry that I had done something rash, impulsive and foolish. I wondered if I had sacrificed a mildly irksome evening of shallow small talk for an evening that had the potential for genuine unpleasantness... if my memory and past experiences served me right. For I suddenly recalled the pointless slanging match and shovings we had gotten into the last time we had seen one another, a long long time ago, after an argument on such a routine topic as the club vs country debate in football had deviated and deteriorated, under Gavin's express direction, into the realms of hurtful personal abuse. But I didn't want my memories and past experiences to serve me correct. Not tonight, I thought. And, besides, did I not have other memories, earlier memories and experiences to draw upon? Earlier and pleasanter memories that needn't, surely, be negated by the tyranny of chronology? Why couldn't those memories be the true ones and the others the chimeras? said Chris, his voice slightly strained with a tone that could almost approximate for beseechment.

Gavin started to speak and something in his calm and measured delivery seemed to suggest that I was right to withold judgment, that I was right to doubt my doubts. He began to ask me a series of questions, enquiring slowly outwards from my thoughts on the venue and its furnishings to the very fundamentals of my livelihood and wellbeing. His interest did not seem feigned and I sensed a genuine attempt at engagement. And with each question it felt as though, I don't know, I was growing warmer and more comfortable, as though a cadmium glow of affection was rising within me and was keen to brim over, to saturate those surroundings, and the whole world to boot.

I remember, said Chris, that Leon passed by, elegantly striding forth to greet yet another guest and I thought to myself how wrong I was—how wrong I was to doubt Leon and his continuous attempts to bring everyone into his life. I could feel that cadmium glow of affection reaching up to the level of my eyes, gently buttressing them with a burning sensation so slight and soft and balmy. And at that moment, over the bar's PA system, that song by Orange Can started to play and Leon looked over his shoulder and flashed me a little smile and, across the table, Gavin was smiling also, and I... I felt like I could just dissolve there and then.

Time does not exist, I remember thinking, echoing words that you yourself had told me just two or three weeks prior. Time does not exist, we just keep changing state. And there we were suddenly back at an earlier state, one I hadn't experienced for so long that I had almost forgotten it could exist. I listened to the first few bars of that song—a song I had only heard once before outside of the confines of headphones; a song I had only heard once before in company and outside of the confines of solitude, when we all watched the eclipse together  that time (do you remember?), up on Leon's roof—and I felt so glad to see these people again. And beneath an ever mounting layer of joy, I sensed the thin immutable stratum of despair receding and becoming more reasonable. These things will pass, it said. But how nice to have enjoyed them.

I better get us a drink, I said to Gavin and went to the bar. Heady, unsteady, and in need of a caesura. And it was whilst I was at the bar, eyes closed for a second, tapping my foot and unconsciously bobbing my head to those few strummed chords of understated majesty, it was then that I felt someone gently squeeze my arm and warn me to be careful—if the sun didn't blind me, this song was good enough to. You'll never guess who it was, Chris paused, less, it seemed, for dramatic effect, and more out of some need for a prompt.

It was Catherine, he said, at length, almost surprising himself.

That glow of affection suddenly spilled over, said Chris, recovering the thread of his narrative, and I hugged her to me, rocking slightly from side to side in disbelief. And I thought of you at that moment and I thought of that story by Maupassant that you once lent me, 'The Minuet'. The one with the old couple dancing in the Jardin du Luxembourg. And I wished you could have been there also—because it felt like everything could begin again, but also as though everything was liable to end. And either eventuality could suffice. It felt so fucking precious. And it felt like it was being wasted on the wrong man, said Chris, his brow furrowed. And I thought to myself this man has always read me with acuity; and I thought to myself, how wonderful and strange to belong in the thoughts and lives of others.

I asked Catherine if she had flown back especially for Leon's birthday, Chris said, and she assured me that that wasn't the case. She had, in fact, moved back to London two months ago. I offered to buy her a drink and, noticing the two pints already in front of me, I then remembered Gavin and all that that entailed. But something told me that such thoughts were irrelevant, they were currencies long since taken out of circulation, they belonged to different states and ages. We weren't living in the time of wergilds. Dynasties of vengeance only destroy themselves. And here we all were: still standing. So I thought, or *felt* rather, that it didn't matter. And I picked up the glasses and motioned to Catherine to follow me.

We slid into the side of the table opposite Gavin. And I won't lie to you, there was an awkward moment or two. It was as if two animals—having been traumatized (and, indeed, distracted) by their being forcibly carried by unfamiliar sets of hands— suddenly realized that they had been dropped down into some cage or sawdust ring, and the animosity and impatience that had been previously focused on their respective carriers' hands disappeared in a heartbeat as they now stared out at each other with a curiosity and a fear born of a completely new and unexpected situation. And Chris laughed.

Most of the conversation was, at first, directed through me, Chris explained. Each in turn—Gavin then Catherine, Catherine then Gavin—would interrogate me about my life, until it became obvious to all that this was what was happening, and Gavin looked across at Catherine and joked that they were acting like a bloody interview panel. And something about his smile and, perhaps, his expansive hand gesture—in which the dim light reflected off his wedding ring, seeming to bathe his entire expression in what I can only describe as reassurance—intimated to myself, certainly, but I'm sure to Catherine as well, that we could relax. And, as if in confirmation, Gavin turned his body slightly to face Catherine, and proceeded to ask her about Japan, believing, as he did, that she still lived there, and had done so for no few years now.

Catherine explained that she had indeed been living in Japan for a long while, but that she had recently (and permanently) returned to London. Her answers were civil but guarded and her own questions seemed, at times, asked only to deflect those put forth by either myself or Gavin. She seemed careworn and wistful in a way I had never previously known her to be, though, of course, I have seen her but little in these last few years.

We spoke about Gavin's wedding which took place last autumn, and he told us about his wife, a Norwegian girl called Else, some years younger than himself, with visible joy. She is an archaeologist and she was away that weekend on a dig somewhere in the Hebrides. They live in Oxford, where they met, Chris went on, Else teaching at the School of Archaeology, Gavin working at the Oxford depot of the same software company he had worked for in London.

Leon joined us and the dynamic of the conversation became, conversely, easier and less stilted under the benign influence of his effusive charm, and yet increasingly laced with tension as the talk veered into reminiscences about the 'old days'.

But nostalgia can be more brutal even than Stalinist purges and the subsequent doctoring of group photos... and our reminiscences largely consisted of us agreeing in unison how 'enjoyable' certain distant occasions had been, skating over details and completely overlooking the odd blanks and holes that littered the pictures we were painting. We said things were 'enjoyable,' said Chris, and we laughed, and we smiled, and we exclaimed *oh my god!* and *I remember that!* And of course we did remember things, but a group consensus is a fallacy, and I found myself in the contrary position of being thoroughly absorbed in my present company and the warmth of our recollections, yet hating the cold, calculating pact of hypocrisy we had all (even, to some extent, Leon) entered into, just to wring out a few drops of present-tense comfort. And in 10 or 20 years would we all remember this night, Leon's birthday, as just another one of the moments of our collective past that we would blandly agree upon as 'enjoyable,' ignoring the huge and rolling panoramas of uneasy context lopped off from either side? And Chris looked at me as though he was genuinely expecting an answer.

We spoke about absent friends, Chris continued, and, of course, your name was mentioned, and Richard's and Dan and Sandra's, and others, I'm sure. And we spoke warmly about these people we missed, summing up their lives in speculative sound bites or sentences, in much the same way we might excrete opinions upon celebrities we haven't really thought about for a while and that, in truth, we know little about: *He's in New York mostly*; *They've got two children now*; *I hear he's writing a book*; *She was always a stylish dresser*; *He still uses that same attaché case*; *I saw her once in John Lewis, but she didn't see me.* Pronouncements that, when isolated thus, sound out empty and banal. And perhaps that's because they were, at their cores, just that: empty and banal. One has only to cut these words away from the animating lifeblood of familiar and genteel faces and gestures to reveal them to be the empty husks they truly are. And is that all we do, really? Sit down around tables and exchange husks? I hope not. We were having a pleasant time, said Chris, and I really resented (and I really resent) the part of my brain that was insinuating (*that does insinuate*) that we were only playing at having a pleasant time. But I do wonder. I do wonder. As soon as you step back from something, as soon as you look back, even at the very most recent occurrences, it does all appear unreal. That is if it appears at all. We have to do it though, don't we? We can't stop doing it. Assessing. Looking back and assessing. And that verb *assess*, it comes from a Latin word meaning 'to sit down.' And it surprises me that we ever get up and *do* anything. In fact, I almost think it logically impossible, because we spend twice as much time looking back and assessing as we do in any *actual* doing. And when you consider that we have to assess the times we've spent assessing, well, then you'll begin to see the paradox I speak of. And if we look back and see unreality, is it any wonder that our presents then become infected with falsity? I'm sorry, said Chris after taking a long draught of his beer, I have recently become plagued by these thoughts and your company, for some reason, seems to bring them out of me.

Gavin stayed for two drinks, but then left to catch his train back to Oxford. He gave everyone a hug goodbye—even Catherine—and the most disingenuous words to slip his lips all evening were when he said to everyone at the table that we must stay in touch and not leave it so long until the next time. Those words rang out hollow to *everyone* and even Leon was caused to murmur—perhaps to himself, perhaps for the benefit of all our ears—that he had the strange feeling that he would not see Gavin again. And I remember thinking that what Leon had muttered could have been applicable if said by any one of us about any one of us. And Chris fell silent. And I became aware of the dull metallic clanging that was emanating from

two barges moored side by side outside the
adjacent Walbrook Wharf. I could see the

hawsers stretching taut and slack as the
strong currents of the ebb tide buffeted
the boats against each other, causing the

freight containers to groan and creak in protest. Containers full of the city's refuse just waiting to be towed out and buried in the landfill sites of Mucking Marshes, thirty miles downriver. And I shivered thinking that it was about the same distance from the centre of London to Brookwood Cemetery. Municipal waste takes many forms, but the radius of removal remains the same.

It was odd, said Chris. I felt that the atmosphere around the table had been a convivial and an open one and that it was not just me who had been brimming over, so to speak, with enthusiasm and affection... But, it was noticeable how some kind of tension lifted on Gavin's departure. It was like we all—all three of us, Leon, Catherine and myself—relaxed back into our natural forms. And I have to say, I felt rather ashamed of myself and disappointed also to see that same relaxation evident in both Catherine and Leon. Especially Leon. He has always been, for me, something approaching a model of sincerity; something approaching a benchmark of hope. Seeing him too relax, as though he had just finished performing a role, was most disheartening. And I began to wonder whether Leon's life of hospitality and inclusion was perhaps more fraught with strains and stresses than anyone else's—a life of constantly hoping everyone would get along; and a life of constant disappointment. Indeed I worry that his innate warmth and optimism will see that he is the first of us to break, to snap irrepressibly and irreversibly at some point. Whereas, perhaps, the likes of you and I, always preparing for and seeing the imminent ruptures of our selves and everything else, in almost everything we say and do, we just go on and on... or as long as we're allowed to, I suppose. And that's the key, isn't it? said Chris, chin rested pensively in his left hand. To realize that everything— *everything*—is a kind of permission granted and that it could be withdrawn at any time, or, rather, Chris smiled mischievously, at any state. And I guess that's why the phrase '...but, of course, I really have no say in the matter' has been rattling around the vaults of my mind with uncommon frequency of late, like an annoying musical ident or radio jingle that plays after any desire I have or any decision I make, branding its message of uncertainty onto everything that I am.

At this point Chris excused himself to head to the gents and, in his absence, I fished into my jacket pocket and took out my mobile phone. I sent a text message to a number I had not used for a long time, but that I had never had the courage to delete. I replaced my phone and leant my head against the glass of the window beside me, letting my eyes drift over the innumerable ripples that played about the river's surface, resembling in no small way the patterns of lines that crease and score the skin upon our fingers and hands. I thought of that saying of Heraclitus about never stepping into the same river twice. And I thought, maybe we are made less of skin and bone, of complex configurations of carbon-based compounds, and more of some ever-flowing formless substance. And I thought that we, like the river, like the waves of the sea, are an energy or force that is constantly moving, constantly flowing through different physical terrains, and also, no less importantly, flowing through different unseen emotional fields. And I thought, perhaps, that though we physically end up breaking on the shore—though physically the bed drains dry—emotionally we flow on and on and on. And then I thought, contradictorily, what if this formless substance is also finite? I thought, what if we wear out this substance slowly and surely during the course of our existences with the thoughts we have, the words we say, and the feelings we share? Each time we impart our emotions, we feel lighter, slightly more euphoric, freer perhaps, and closer to the ultimate end we all fear so much, but so desperately crave. We become happier as we shed our ballast and begin to move with greater autonomy. But we are, in some indeterminable way, diminished, spent, and closer to extinction. How I longed, at times, for such complete annihilation.

The pane reverberated with the rumbling of a train departing from the station overhead. In company and in conversation, one soon became inured to the noises of the arrivals and departures into and out of Cannon Street station, but when on one's own, or when the pub had fallen silent, the noise was most ominous. I remembered an epileptic acquaintance of mine once describing his fits as being preceded by, sometimes, a sensation resembling that of a light breeze blowing gently across the temples and as if beneath the epidermis; or, at other times, by an imagined sound of thunder rolling out somewhere high above. He said these strange heralds were termed auras by the doctors and scientists who studied these sorts of phenomena.

Medication could keep the condition in check, for the most part, but occasionally he would hear the noise of a nearby, but out-of-sight train or juggernaut or the sound of metal shutters and grilles being rolled across shopfronts or garage doors, and he would briefly be transported back into that state of foreboding, fearing the proximity of a paroxysm.

Chris returned and took his seat. He looked out the window for a minute or two, staring at or through the bridge and its four squat sets of legs that made it resemble the form of some pond-dwelling larvae risen briefly to the surface. You know, Chris eventually resumed, his voice hushed and hesitant, I thought that I had had a good time on Saturday night. I thought that something had been rediscovered and reaffirmed. I am sure that I had felt, in some indefinable way, on a more level footing—that my friends and experiences of the past were proving themselves to be not sinkholes threatening

to destroy my present existence, but were instead sound and solid foundations on which all my current concerns could play out at will. But as we have talked things over this afternoon, I have come to see that all of these affectionate feelings may only have been born out of the peculiar circumstance of hearing a particular favourite song at a particular time and in particular company. And that everything else was just the usual palaver of playacting, preservation and politics. That perhaps the evening had just been one of undeniable awkwardness and devastation. A reminder to all of us who were there that it is the pain that is the constant and that all else is merely a deviation from it. Comfort will always be illusory; and a common experience nothing short of impossible. And Chris banged his clenched fist lightly but firmly on the table causing the condiments, hiding between the folds of the menus, to knock into each other as they jumped a little in fright or consternation. I continue to amaze myself, Chris went on, rubbing the corners of his eyes in turn with the knuckle of his left index finger, I continue to amaze myself, he repeated through a yawn, I continue to amaze myself at my own capacity to vacillate so wildly between a complete and utter conviction in the necessity of the love and bonds I have for and to my fellow companions in this world, and a competing suspicion, no less absolute, of there being no worth or truth at all to any of my relations.

I understood Chris all too well, recognizing not only some of my own sentiments in his confession, but even hearing a familiarity in the very wording of his phrases, as though I had said them myself at some forgotten time, or in some vanished dimension. Our personalities were, I had realized, too similar to provide either of us with any great distraction or reassurance. And that was, perhaps, why we got on so well and also why we could go great lengths of time without seeing one another.

I don't know, sighed Chris. It's like I said earlier—the thought occurred to me very early on during the course of that evening that I was the wrong man, that it should have been someone else witnessing and experiencing those events. To feel like an actor in your own life—that has got to be one of the most undermining feelings possible... but, of course, I really have no say in the matter.

I walked away from the pub that day, instinctively heading west, perhaps drawn to Blackfriars Bridge, or maybe towards the fast-setting sun which beckoned my Icarus-wings. I wound my way through the caged passageway across the Cory container yard

at Walbrook Wharf, beneath the enormous toytown hoist, and out on to Three Cranes Walk. Here, just east of Southwark Bridge, I saw that a small crowd had gathered on the embankment. It seemed that they were watching the fishing endeavours of a cormorant that had recently emerged from below the surface with an eel wriggling and

writing in its beak. The cormorant—black, ancient, pterodactylesque—struggled to maintain its grip on the eel, a barb of silver whose scales occasionally reflected the rainbow spectrum latent in the dipping sun's perpetual rays. The cormorant snapped its beak open and shut, trying to manoeuvre its catch in such a way that it could be swallowed down whole. The eel, meanwhile, flexed and contorted those parts of its body and tail that were not pinioned in the bird's vicelike hold. The cormorant lost the eel only to dive down into the grey-brown murk of the Thames and re-emerge with its prey captive and squirming once

119

more. This happened several times and the small crowd of onlookers on the bankside followed the progress upriver towards the bridge. Each time the cormorant dropped its catch into the water there was an audible gasp from members of the crowd. And each time the cormorant surfaced with the eel once more in its beak there were cheers. The more time this spectacle repeated itself, the more invested the crowd became in this timeless ritual. We have to keep watching, we have to keep relaying, until the inevitable denouement has played out. Some people laughed as the cormorant wrestled with the heaving silvery tongue that would not be quieted. Half-swallowed half a dozen times, the eel thrashed out at gullet walls and keening stomach acids and somehow slipped free. After five or six minutes, however, the curtain came down on this impromptu performance piece. And as the last hint of silver slithered down the cormorant's throat, a small round of unsolicited applause broke out amongst the soon dispersing spectators on the riverbank.

I guess it's in our nature to take sides. I guess we also want to identify ourselves with victors, survivors and success. But before that small crowd parted, as swiftly and unfussily as it had surely formed, some of the strangers looked about at each

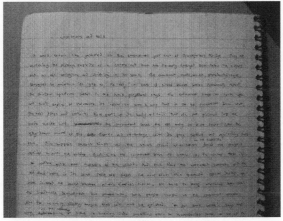

other, and they caught sight of each other's expressions of satisfaction and contentment and I'm sure that they felt ashamed. They had all managed to see one creature's desperate struggle for life as a comedy. And even if they had seen it as a tragedy, did

that make any difference? I certainly felt ashamed. I had not cheered or applauded. But I had stopped. I had stopped to watch. To take everything on board. To absorb it and, quite possibly, to make use of it for my own ends. Municipal waste and waste management indeed.

I continued on to Southwark Bridge which, in the setting sun, looked like the kind of bridge one might see painted on the background of the enormous sets of *ballets russes*. The distinctive combination of its almost-turquoise green and just-shy-of-golden yellow was one that I could never recall being used elsewhere for any other thing—stationary mastheads, company logos, football club strips, hotel lobby furniture, train seat upholstery, flags of states and nations, fleets of aircraft, confectionary wrappers, the livery of servants—until it hit me for the first time there and then. The only other place I had ever seen this combination of colours was

on the plumage of a certain species of tropical parrot: the blue-and-yellow macaw. In some way buoyed or disorientated by this revelation and the bridge's new and unlikely connection to an elsewhere and an otherland, I turned immediately left at the end of Fruiterers Passage, a kind of tiled fractal of what arced above it, and ascended the steps to cross Southwark Bridge—the least used of the City's bridges, standing over the Thames like an overlooked and magical escape route from unrealized torments. The lampposts that adorned the bridge stood with arms outstretched like

ministers performing
extravagant blessings
(or like criminals strung
out upon Golgotha)
and as I crossed the
bridge, feeling oddly
unburdened, I felt
an unexpected and
mechanical palpitation around my chest.
It was my phone. I sat down in one of the
stone recesses of the bridge to look at the
incoming message. Assessment, I thought.
Reassessment, I corrected myself, smiling
wanly. And I got up and continued on my
way.

That night I dreamt, as I have done once
or twice before in the past, of taking a train
journey down to East Sussex, the train then
rattling out along the coast to somewhere
near Folkestone where, after a halt for
unspecified reasons, the train continued on,

on and over the Channel Bridge. The bridge curved out above the waters, stretching into distances so vast that one could never see, at any one point in time, the entire length of its span.

I remember the train journey with as much clarity and emotion—probably much more—as I do many of the trips and holidays I have taken in my so-called real life. When I think back to that train ride and the darkening greens of the countryside rolling past outside of the windows, I am filled with an immense sadness and a sense of loss for something I could never be expected to fully articulate or understand.

It was as though a whole other world had been glimpsed and denied. I remember no other characters or faces from that dream, the whole infrastructure seemed to be geared to ferry me and me alone. But I never once felt alone. The distant sun remained always above the horizon and at certain angles and turns of the track, the carriages of the train would be flooded with a gentle warmth which never entirely vanished.

The only certainty I have ever carried with me is that I will one day ride that train again.

My recurring dream of the Channel Bridge—although it is not so much a recurring dream as an occasionally-glimpsed but nevertheless consistent feature of a world that I have often explored if little remembered—has mutated into my waking world, it seems, albeit transferring to the eastern hemisphere of the globe, and becoming a road rather than a railway bridge. I am talking about the Qingdao Haiwan Bridge in the Shandong Province

of China that was completed in 2011, becoming the longest marine bridge in the world at over 26 miles in length across the gulf of the Jiaozhou Bay. When I first saw a picture of this incredible feat of construction, embedded in a news story next to the log-in box for my email account, I was astonished, for the image was an almost entirely faithful reproduction of what I had experienced in my dreams. I didn't know whether to be perturbed or reassured, to feel blessed or cursed, but somehow or other, as that ice-hot dagger of déjà vu began to diffuse, I did fall under the impression that the world was beginning to make more sense.

When

Our tendency is, perhaps, nowadays (and, really, always, since the birth of mythology), to think of a never ending task as something absurd and meaningless; a punishment even. And yet many also think of the never ending, the timeless, the eternal, if you will, as the last great hope (or certainty). And these thoughts are far from mutually exclusive. I guess our memories provide similar comforts and torments. And I guess too that they may also be seen as never ending tasks, each recollection providing a fresh coat of paint over the rusting girders of memory's framework; each recollection letting the intricate exploits of engineering be seen in ever differing lights.

And so it happens, perhaps, that as my wife and I drive home from Scotland on an autumnal day peppered with sunshine and showers, I come to think about how durable loss is, the rods and cones of our eyes forever processing photons emitted from moments already spent. And I think, perhaps, as we near the shores of the Lothians, leaving behind us the extinct but still looming volcanic mass of the Lomond Hills, that if we are physically constrained to be trapped in the absurdity of a time already vanished then maybe we can also be simultaneously liberated into a present by something within us that is independent of an extraordinary variety of biochemical processes, and I wonder if that something might be our emotions, and I wonder if that something might be love. And if we are anything but cast-iron in our doubts about the existence of such forces, then we must surely begin to suspect the sheer ludicrousness of the notion of almost anything, be it animal, vegetable or mineral—let alone something as intangibly complex, divergent and harmonious as a relationship—as having a definitive finishing line.

—2014—

End

J ames Wilson is the author of two volumes of prose poems, *All the Colours Fade* and *The Song Remains the Same* (both Miami, FL: The Hippocrene Society, 2012) and the essay collection *Images of the Afterlife in Cinema* (London: Duchy of Lambeth, 2011). James is co-editor and contributor to the anthology, *Flaws of Oblivion* (The Hippocrene Society, 2014). He is also the translator of two volumes of the French writer Guy de Maupassant: *To the Sun* and *The Foreign Soul & The Angelus*. His prose fiction has appeared in the journals *The Use of English* and *Snow*. He lives in London where he works for the Swedenborg Society.

Made in the USA
Charleston, SC
05 July 2014